Fun in Every Alley
Seoul Stories

by David Ritchie

NulBom

To the people of the Republic of Korea,

who gave a foreigner a new and cozy home.

Ajumma's letter of recommendation

Dear readers:

This book is a sympathetic but sharp-eyed portrait of Seoul, and especially the little things: corner groceries, gingko leaves, and life in a Yeogwan.

Look at Seoul through a friendly foreigner's eyes, and you may never see Seoul in the same way again.

I should know ··· I'm the one who keeps Seoul running, right?

From Ajumma

Preface

The author would like to thank Mr. Cho Yoo-hyun for printing the articles collected here, and the staff of Seoul Scope magazine for all their efforts toward getting this book into print.

Thanks are due also to Seoul Scope's readers, who made this column a success.

Opinions expressed in this work are the author's unless otherwise noted.

Readers should bear in mind that many of these essays are carefree fantasias on life in Seoul, not factual reportage, and therefore should not be taken too seriously.

Also, Korean readers will understand that light verse in English does not translate easily into Korean.

David Woodfin Ritchie

Contents

5. Seoul, 'the Miracle Wonderful'

6. Nonetheless, Seoul & its people—Not Understandable

7. I Do This Kind of Work, Anyway Sorry!

1

SEOUL, WE CAN'T
STOP LOVING YOU

Welcome to the Neighborhood!

Mr. Rogers has made a career of welcoming people to his neighborhood. Care to see the corner of Seoul that I call home?

I live in Pilun-dong, next to Sajik Park and within sight of the ancient palace at Gyeongbokgung. From my window, I see the whole range of Korean history and culture at a glance – from palace rooftops to the huge outdoor display screen just beyond. The neighborhood starts bustling about 6 am. Delivery men arrive in their trucks, with goods for stores. Sometimes the trucks play little tunes as they back up. (Before coming to Korea, I had never heard a wheeled vehicle play 'Highland Laddie.') One by one, the shops open. The Grocery Lady tries to engage me in conversation, even though she knows no English and my Korean is awful. But you can accomplish a lot with smiles and gestures!

The Fruit Stand Man is great. He sells the most delicious pears in Asia, and keeps smiling even on the coldest days.

The News stand Lady is a welcome sight too. Her shop has a little grill so you can buy a bean-paste cake to go with your newspaper. (Try to find that in New York!)

Marching through it all is the Cardboard Box Man. He collects used cardboard boxes, collapses them, and hauls them away on his cart. He announces his approach by rapping on a pair of shears. Kling! Kling! Kling!

Then there is The Complete Store. Practically anything you might want is here, in a space not much bigger than a phone booth. Remember how Doctor Who's time machine, the TARDIS, was much bigger on the inside than on the outside? You wonder if this shopkeeper took lessons from him!

Pilun-dong is home now, in a way that my old neighborhood in Virginia never was. Can you say "cozy"? Can you say "fascinating"?

Kling! Kling! Kling!

Bountiful Bookstores!

If I'm neither at home nor at the office, chances are you'll find me in one of Seoul's great bookstores. Whether or not you're fluent in Korean, you will find something of interest there!

You'll find beach books, to be sure. But if you go to a Korean bookstore looking for a beach book, one has to wonder why you came to Korea in the first place, instead of Virginia Beach or Santa Monica.

So look at the rest of the stock! You'll be amazed what is there!

At one bookstore downtown, I found a handsome illustrated set of Gibbon's Decline and Fall of the Roman Empire, C. S. Lewis's Studies in Words, and an enormous dictionary of folklore, legend and mythology that has seen a lot of use in my book research.

Another store, underground near the Uljiro 1-ga subway station, has yielded a bonanza of titles, from Plutarch's

Lives to Walter Lord's A Night To Remember, about the sinking of the Titanic.

Don't forget the used-book stores! At one shop near Itaewon, I found a complete four-volume set of George Orwell's collected journalism, for little more than pocket change. Another shop near City Hall proudly displayed an anthology of Fearless Fosdick's adventures. (Okay, comic-strip trivia lovers: who was Fosdick's long-suffering fiancee?)

And then there are translations of Korean literature. History, folktales ··· the selection is endless. One of my favorites is the story of the puppy who captured three tigers with nothing more than a little grease and a rope.

Mysteries, histories, magazines, comics they're all waiting for you in the bookstores of Seoul. Perfect for that long flight home!

Fabulous Food!

Everyone loves food, right? So everyone should also love Seoul, which has something to delight every restaurantgoer's taste. Italian, Mexican, Indian, Afghan, American, Russian, seafood, beef, vegetarian ⋯ you'll find all these cuisines here, and more!

But Seoul is a Korean city, and of course its great glory is Korean food. If this is your first visit to Korea, then you're probably never had genuine Korean food before. Now, where do you go for the good stuff?

Great Korean meals are everywhere. You just have to do a little looking to find the best places. Here, it helps to inquire of Korean friends, or someone at your hotel.

Ask, "Where's a good place for Samgyetang?" – and in a few minutes you'll be seated in a cozy restaurant on a side street, with a piping-hot bowl of the luscious chicken stew in front of you.

The really good restaurants don't always have flashy signs,

impressive facades, or lush foliage in the hallway. Just as often, they are unassuming little places which ordinarily you wouldn't give a second look! One of my favorites is all but camouflaged in a little alley near Gyeongbokgung.

Restaurants here don't skimp on the side dishes, either. You'll find a stunning array of side dishes, from kimchi (Korea's spicy pickled vegetable dish) to cold soups.

One word of caution: if you have the sensitive Western digestion, then go easy on the hot stuff. Even Koreans sometimes overindulge, and pay for it later. As I write, one Korean friend is recovering from an encounter with a super-spicy squid dish!

But visiting Westerners still have plenty of great Korean dishes to choose from. Galbi to Gimbap, Bibimbap to Bulgogi - enjoy them while you're here!

To Market, To Market!

Now that mild weather is here, make time for that great Korean attraction – the outdoor market!

If you're never visited Korea's outdoor markets before, get ready for a new experience. In the USA and Canada, shopping is boring and sterile by comparison. There, everything is neatly ordered and labeled and packaged, and generally made as dull as possible.

But in Korean markets, shopping is what it should be bustling, aromatic, noisy, and fun!

Perhaps the best thing about outdoor markets here is, you never know when and where you will find one. Walk around the corner, and suddenly you're in a long line of open-air stores and stalls stretching as far as the eye can see.

Every square inch of this outdoor bazaar is packed with merchandise. The variety is astonishing. Linen to legumes, pears to poultry, boots to bath towels: you'll find them all here, and millions of other things besides!

Please understand. This is not a spacious, tranquil mall on the American model. It's more like five malls squeezed into a tenth the volume of one! At an outdoor market, there is almost always a crowd. People bounce off one another like billiard balls. Children yell. Live seafood swims and jumps in tanks and tubs. But no one seems to mind, not even when a delivery man on a motorbike roars through. And if you seek a brief respite from crowding, chances are a nice, relaxing coffee shop is only a few steps away.

My favorite haunts are the produce stands. Enormous, juicy Asian pears, gigantic strawberries, luscious melons, and big sweet apples. Love them!

So make time for a market. Buy a waffle from a vendor if you like. (Waffles here are great; huge, hot, and dripping with butter and honey) Then munch away as you stroll. You'll come away with colorful memories, if not an armload of merchandise!

The Side Street Show!

A few steps off the main thoroughfares of Seoul, you suddenly find yourself in a maze of tiny lanes and alleys. That's where things really start to get lively!

Seoul's side streets are home to everything from billiard halls to barber shops. It's like a gigantic used-book sale where you may find Vertebrate Paleontology next to Ivanhoe, and you never know what you'll encounter next!

One thing you're sure to encounter is traffic. And beware: never presume that cars will yield to pedestrians! When you hear that unmistakable roar behind you, better step out of the way and let that motorist by.

On the other hand, side street traffic can be entertaining too. Near my apartment, for example, an intersection has just about the area of a suburban living room in the USA And even this area is often reduced by parked cars.

Enter a cement mixer. One night on the way home from the office, I found one right in the middle of that tiny

inter-section. The driver apparently had made a mistake and was trying to turn around.

And he did it! Deftly, he wheeled the metal monster around, missing cars around him by the width of a drinking straw, and proceeded up the hill unscathed. It was like watching an elephant perform a pirouette in a phone booth!

So if you have a chance, explore the side streets. It's great entertainment, and completely free of charge!

Jolly, Jumbled Jonggak!

Seoul is a city of neighborhoods. Insa-dong, Itaewon – each one has its special character and charm.

But of all Seoul's neighborhoods, my favorite is Jonggak. Also known as Jonggak, it's a colorful and fascinating jumble of shops and schools, restaurants and retailers, bakeries and bookstores, all squeezed into an area barely bigger than a football field!

Whatever you're looking for, from Hanbok(Korean traditional dress) to hamburgers, it's probably here in Jonggak. And if you want to see what this city is all about, just walk around the area near the subway station. It's wonderful for Seoul-watching!

Stroll through the neighborhood at lunchtime, and here is a sample of what you may see:

A gigantic portrait of Elvis Presley dancing.

Ladies carrying tiny, pampered pooches in their arms.

A delivery man on a motorbike, carrying a tower of eggs in cartons.

An outdoor display screen showing a video of trick billiard shots.

Two octopi having a battle in a seafood restaurant's tank.

Now, a word of advice: Jonggak can be hectic indeed around lunchtime. Seoulites are used to getting bumped and jostled on the sidewalk. But if you're a visitor, maybe you'd better visit in the morning or mid-afternoon to avoid the crowds!

And if you want to relax a moment, try one of Jonggak's countless coffee shops. They are little havens of tranquillity in Seoul's hopping hub!

Wonderful Walnuts!

In winter, note those little street stands selling hot fried dough in the shape of walnuts. The stands, set up by the subway entrances, send a sweet fragrance wafting down the stairs.

A bagful of these little pastries costs next to nothing and is one of the great traditions of Seoul, like hot-dog stands on the streets of New York.

Now let me get out the calculator and do a little figuring. If each dough walnut is a cubic inch in volume ⋯ and half the population of South Korea buys one bagful per year (a fair assumption) ⋯ and each bag contains maybe 10 walnuts ⋯ that's enough to fill a cube five stories tall!

Whew. And the magnitude of that business! Cheap as the treats are, some cities run on less money per year than Korea spends on dough walnuts!

So Korea's dough walnuts teach two lessons. One, little things add up. Two, there is money in even the simplest

product, if demand and distribution are right.

Think about that for a while. And while you do, enjoy a bag of dough walnuts. You may not have a commercial brainstorm, but they go great with coffee on a cold day!

The Great Korean Coffee Shop!

It's a cold day in Seoul. While doing around the city, you want to drink something hot and relax in a nice soft chair for a few minutes.

Well, you're in the right place. One of Seoul's great institutions is (drum roll, please) ⋯ the coffee shop!

This is not a coffee shop on the American model. A USA coffee shop is apt to be a bleak place with cold, hard seats and counter, and dismal little slices of pie withering under a plastic cover.

But not in Seoul! They do things differently here ⋯ and beautifully!

A coffee shop in Seoul may look like the lobby of a luxury hotel. You get a delightfully soft seat that seems big enough for Paul Bunyan.

The interior is bright and cheerful. Just walking in the door makes you feel better. And the coffee is splendid. Your only difficult moment may be selecting a coffee from that monumental menu!

No matter where you go, a coffee shop is nearby. Toss a paper airplane, and there is a good chance it will sail into a coffee shop. And chances are the coffee and atmosphere there will be great!

What does this happy experience cost? Not much.

A cup of rich, satisfying coffee at one of Seoul's cozy coffee shops may cost 3,000 won or so ⋯ less than a newsmagazine. And instead of gloomy news, you get tasty refreshment in a relaxing environment.

Maybe I'll see you at a coffee shop soon. I'm the foreigner with glasses and a graying beard, way over in the corner!

Meet the Kims!

You will make many friends in Seoul ⋯ and many of them will be named Kim.

If you removed all the Kims from Korea, there would be few people left. I forget who wrote that. Maybe John Steinbeck.

I's an exaggeration. But not by much! 'Kim' is to Korea roughly what 'Jones' is to Wales. And just as the Welsh traditionally refer to individual Joneses as 'Jones the Such-and-such', I tend to do the same with Kims. Meet a few of them:

Mr. Kim the Troubleshooter. He is a great source of practical advice, and a good friend to awkward foreigners. When a significant problem arises, I go to him!

Mr. Kim the Gregarious. Kind and outgoing, he resembles a Korean Milton Berle and even has a similar grin.

Mr. Kim the Explainer. He has a brief, coherent explanation for almost anything. He really should have been a diplomat.

Mr. Kim the Sage. A prodigiously well-informed man, this Mr. Kim knows about everything from restaurants to real estate. It's as if he carries the Library of Congress around in his head!

Miss Kim the Baseball Fan. A tiny, cheerful young woman, she appears to weigh little more than the baseball. Whatever happens, she keeps smiling. If only the world had more people like her!

Miss Kim the Computer Expert. I'm be lost without her. When something goes wrong with my computer, It's Miss Kim to the rescue. (The mathematical and mechanical abilities that men are supposed to have were left out of me. Now I know what happened. Miss Kim got them instead!)

The Kims are wonderful. I love them. No one has better personal Kim-istry!

Those Terrific Taxis!

No, that wasn't a jet interceptor that just roared past you. That was a Seoul taxi – a unique phenomenon. (How can you tell the difference? The jet has wings. Somehow, a Seoul taxi manages to fly without them!)

Seriously, Seoul's taxis are a great way to get around the city. Rates are economical. The drivers know their way around. And they are marvelously patient with tourists – especially this gray-bearded foreigner with the funny accent! A taxi ride in Korea can be a marvelous intercultural experience, too. You might wind up sitting in a Korean taxi, listening to a recording of "Havah Nagilah" sung in French! (That actually happened to me in Incheon.)

Seoul taxis are clean. The driver may even wear white gloves. This is a refreshing change from (ahem) a certain other country I could name, where I once climbed into a taxi and found myself amidst discarded drink cans and snack-food bags.

A taxi ride across Seoul – say, from Jonggak to Gangnam – is a good way to see the city. Along the way, you notice a lot of intriguing stores, galleries and other attractions that you would miss on a subway ride!

Besides, your driver may provide you with a delightful memory of Seoul. On a ride to Sajik-dong one night, my driver, a lover of classical music, unexpectedly asked, "Do you like Mozart?"

In no other city has a taxi driver ever asked me such a question!

Gangnam Kaleidoscope!

You hear a lot about tourist attractions in downtown Seoul. But There's life south of the river, too! Just cross the bridge, and you're in Gangnam – a big, lively place with something for everyone!

Gangnam is a new part of Seoul. Most of it has arisen in just the last 20 years. So Gangnam is young, vibrant, and filled with almost anything you might want, from outdoor markets to optical shops. My apartment is in Gangnam. It's a colorful (and sometimes pleasantly mystifying!) place to live. Walking down the street toward the health club, I pass a coffee shop that advertises 'Koffie engebak'. The 'koffie' part seems clear enough. But 'engebak'? My dictionary doesn't list that one!

Stroll down the street in Gangnam. It's fascinating. You may find yourself face to face with anything from an outdoor sculpture of a giant toad (really!) to a polystyrene portrait bust of some noble Roman in an art-supplies store. Imperial

Caesar, dead and turned to plastic! In Gangnam, you just don't know what you may encounter next. Gangnam is like an unorganized bookstore where you find Sidney Sheldon next to Shakespeare, or cookbooks next to car manuals.

Gangnam is a great place for restaurants. Everything is here, from traditional Korean cuisine to Western-style fried chicken. Fine bakeries, too. One of them sells the kind of whole-grain bread you dream about.

So check out Gangnam. It may not have the ancient solemnity and beauty of a palace. But It's an unforgettable place to visit. Maybe I'll see you here, trying to find out what 'engebak' means!

Wealth and Wisdom!

One thing I like about Seoul is the way it handles wealth – very wisely. Seoul has its share of extremely rich people. I met one of them a couple of years ago. Though possessed of fantastic wealth, he looked like any other salaryman. Passing him on the street, you wouldn't notice anything extraordinary about him. That's how Seoul's upper crust handles its riches. People here don't flaunt wealth. It's a pleasant change from the United States, where the well-to-do all but wave their greenbacks in your face.

You may or may not believe what follows, but here, according to an Associated Press report on my desk, are prices wealthy Americans are actually paying for various items these days: $10,000 for gold-plated faucets, $4,200 for a handbag, $2,300 for a pillow filled with goose down, $1,000 for door hinges. Remember, these figures are not in South Korean won. These are dollar amounts. In won, they would be reasonable. In dollars ⋯ well, something is rotten in the land of the $10,000 faucet. If everyday household fixtures bear such price tags, you can imagine what relative luxuries cost!

Now contrast this USA extravagance with Seoul, where simple and inexpensive pleasures still abound: a hike in the hills ⋯ a bicycle ride along the river ⋯ a nice Galbi dinner at a cozy corner restaurant. And here, clothes are not a sure guide to personal assets. That gentleman in the slightly shabby suit over there may be pulling in $1 million per year.

Seoul's wealthy have the good taste to keep their riches under wraps, so to speak, instead of trying to dazzle you with diamonds or lighting $50 cigars with $100 bills. In New York, a limousine is nearly as long as the Titanic. A Seoul limo, on the other hand, is maybe 30 cm longer than an ordinary sedan.

American cities, they say, are becoming places for either the very rich or the very poor. Seoul, on the other hand, still has plenty of room in the middle ⋯ happily for me, because That's right where my pleasures and I belong!

Home, Sweet Yeogwan!

Every night after work, I walk home to a Yeogwan. That's a traditional Korean inn. It's marvelous! Come with me for a look inside.

Rent is modest. For about USA $30 per night, I get a quiet, cozy room with private bath and maid service.

The Yeogwan has air-conditioning for the summer months, and a convenience store downstairs for late-night purchases. Everything I need, from a pharmacy to a fruit stand, is just a short walk away.

The family that runs the Yeogwan is great. They speak little English, and my Korean is lousy. But they don't seem to mind ⋯ and besides, you can communicate much with a few words and facial expressions.

Then there are the lovely details that you don't find in the West. The first thing I see on entering the lobby is a huge aquarium full of ornamental carp. It's a wonderfully restful sight.

When I get to my room, there is a nice soft 'Yo' (Korean mattress) waiting. I unfold it and soon am sound asleep.

Even better is what I do not find waiting at the Yeogwan. For example:

No junk mail! You don't know what a bane it is until you escape it.

No phone messages! There's no answering machine at the Yeogwan. I hope there never will be. Leave business at the office!

No car alarms! You don't hear that ear-splitting electronic howl every five minutes outside your window, as you would in America. At the Yeogwan, you can actually sleep at night! What a concept!

If you prefer Western-style accommodations, That's okay. Korea has splendid hotels of that kind. But Yeogwan living suits me fine. That's why, among all those Korean guests, There's a happy, bearded foreigner at the end of the hall!

Yea for the Yo!

Ever notice how furniture affects behavior? American homes are built around their entertainment centers. Russian households are focused on the kitchen table. And in Korea, you will encounter the 'Yo effect'.

If you stay at a Yeogwan, or Korean traditional inn, you'll probably find a yo waiting for you – a thin mattress like the Japanese futon, with a thick blanket for cover on chilly nights.

Just unfold the Yo, stretch out, and relax. Lightweight and firm, the Yo is the most comfortable form of bedding I have ever used.

And once you lie down on a Yo, you'll probably find it difficult to get up again. It's not that you can't arise from a Yo. You just don't want to.

When the brain tells the rest of the body at 7 am. 'Get up and start the day', all the limbs shout back, 'shut up! We like it here!' That is the yo effect.

For saving space, nothing beats a Yo. When not in use, a yo big enough for a fullback folds up into a volume barely bigger than a briefcase.

Korean pillows are great too. Western pillows tend to be filled with plastic-fiber stuff that makes them feel (as the old joke goes) like giant marshmallows. They support your head, but that's about all.

But many pillows in Korea are filled with grain husks instead. So when you rest your head on them, you hear a soft, soothing rustle, like wind through the trees. Korean pillows even give you the bonus of a relaxing sound!

So, three cheers for the Yo! Try one while you're here, and see if you prefer it to those metal-frame barges in Western bedrooms!

Soju Serenade!

Scholars will tell you that Korean society is rooted in Confucianism, or Buddhism, or shamanism. Actually, it floats on a sea of soju. The ubiquitous Korean vodka, soju is not really made to be savored. Instead, it is meant to be knocked back, shot after shot.

Then the singing starts. Koreans like to sing, and a few ounces of soju will bring out the Pavarotti in the typical Mr. Park.

Usually, the singing is confined to a restaurant, bar or club. But sometimes it spills out into the streets, and ⋯ well, here is an example.

A gentleman in his cups stationed himself in front of my apartment building one night and decided to serenade Gangnam. His voice wasn't bad, but the hour was late, and people were trying to sleep.

To make matters worse, his singing annoyed a neighbor's dog, which began barking in reply. But the singer was too

far gone to care. In the United States, someone might lean out the window and scream. But my Korean neighbors were more discreet. I heard the sound of footsteps upstairs, as of someone walking to the phone. Moments later, the bright lights of a police car appeared outside.

The singing stopped. The car departed. The dog shut up. And peace returned to our little corner of Gangnam. The singer, I guess, wound up sleeping it off at the station.

You may hear a few soju serenades while in Korea. But there are worse things to hear in the middle of the night – like midnight gunfire in DC or Baltimore.

Give me a soju serenader in Seoul any day!

Charming Charlie the Jindo!

Korea's distinctive dog breed is the Jindo. A sturdy, medium-sized dog known for its big round head and curly tail, the Jindo is also famous for its phenomenal devotion to its owner. A Jindo separated from its owner will travel hundreds of kilometers for a reunion. So the story goes, anyway.

The downside is that Jindos are not really charming dogs. As a rule, Jindos love their owners but take a dim view of anyone else. Fierce and independent, the Jindo makes a great watchdog but wins no awards for amiability. At least, I wouldn't try to pet one!

Yet there is an exception. I call him Charlie, because I don't know his real name. Charlie is that great rarity, a sweet-tempered Jindo.

Charlie presides over a parking lot near my office. Passersby see Charlie draped over a motorcycle, gazing benevolently at everyone, apparently convinced that all's right with the world!

One could scarcely call Charlie a guard dog, because It's hard to imagine Charlie actively defending anything. If he could talk, he might say, "who am I to tell you what to do?"

How Charlie got his sunny disposition is unknown. I can't see any trace of a golden retriever in his ancestry. In any case, there was a little testimonial to Charlie's good cheer at the parking lot one night.

The lot was closed. Charlie wasn't there. But in his absence, someone had left a big, grinning stuffed dog.

If the real Charlie wasn't available, that was the next best thing!

2

CAN THE MAYOR OF SEOUL
KNOW ABOUT THIS?

Korea's Top 10

Once I asked students at a private school to name 10 things they liked about Korea. High on the list was, 'It's easy to get a drink.'?

Here is my own '10 Best' list about the Asian land I now call home.

1. **Safe streets** : After living in the US urban jungle, I'm grateful for the relative safety of Korea. At night, I walk around with fairly large sums of cash, but no great fear of robbery. Try doing that in DC!

2. **Kimchi** : Korea's national food – spicy pickled cabbage. It's an acquired taste, but more healthful than the fatty US diet.

3. **Bookstores** : Anything from beach books to Aristophanes. Amazing!

4. **Radio** : You never know what you'll hear next: Bach, Bing Crosby, or Pink Floyd.

5. **Store signs** : Unpredictable. 'Turtle Jewelry', 'Flash

Baekery', 'Beettle Beer' And so on, indefinitely.

6. Trains : The Saemaul express train between Seoul and Busan is as good as America's Metroliner but less than half the fare.

7. Waffles : A mere 1000 won(about 1 dollar) buys the waffle of your dreams – big, crisp and dripping with butter and honey!

8. Coffee shops : Korea's coffee shops are the antithesis of those cold plastic counters in US diners. Here, you get cozy chairs, nice music, and a good menu.

9. Mandu : Another traditional Korean food – big steamed dumplings stuffed with meat or kimchi. It's a filling (and economical) lunch ⋯ like giant ravioli!

10. Your choice : What's your favorite?

Seoul's Not Cute ··· and I'm Not Sorry!

You can apply a lot of adjectives to Seoul. Powerful. Dynamic. Enormous. Productive. Brilliant. Beautiful. Historic. Stately. Resilient. And so on.

But you cannot call Seoul cute. And for that, I'm grateful.

For the last ten years or so, a wave of cuteness – really sickening cuteness – has been sweeping the world.

Saccharine cartoons, icky-poo dolls, and animal toys in the image of human babies(singing in eerie falsetto voices) have made me wonder which appeal is worse: the violence and splattered blood of videogames, or the feigned innocence and charm of Cutesylvania.

Well, I'm glad to say that the aforementioned wave of ultra-cuteness has swept over Korea without much effect. A certain kitten does peer blank-faced at me in stores all over Seoul, but I'm fond of cats, so at least the little critter is tolerable.

Let other cultures and cities put on a cutesy face if they

wish. But Seoul? Never!

Seoul is a roaring tiger, not an insipid kitten, bird or puppy. And I, for one, wouldn't have Seoul any other way! ROOOOOAAAAARRRRR!

Seoul Needs a Nickname!

Great cities tend to have nicknames. New York is 'the Big Apple', Chicago is 'the Windy City', Boston is 'the Hub(as in 'hub of the universe')', Tokyo is 'the Tangerine'. And one tourist guide describes Jakarta as the 'Durian' – that famous Asian fruit that smells bad but tastes delicious.

Now, what about Seoul?

While teaching at a hagwon(private school) one year, I asked students if Seoul had a nickname. They said no. Apparently Seoul does not have an affectionate, familiar name.

So maybe It's time to find a nickname for Korea's capital. Here are some suggestions:

- **The Big Mandu** : A huge, hot dumpling stuffed with all kinds of ingredients. Appropriate image, isn't It's
- **Ajumma** : That means 'Auntie.' It's the word for the hard-working middle-aged ladies who run Seoul's

shops and restaurants. Ajumma keeps the city going. Why not name it after her?

- **The Pear** : Big, sweet and beautiful!
- **Tiger City** : Maybe Hodori(cartoon tiger mascot of the 1988 Olympics) has a relative who could perform the same job for Seoul.
- **The Magpie** : Bold and loud – and already a beloved symbol of Korea!
- **The Crane** : But first we'll have to decide which kind: the feathered crane, or the construction crane?

Tiger Tales!

Every country has animal fables, and favorite animal characters. France has Chanticleer the rooster. Canada has the Loup-garou, something like a Gallicized werewolf. The United States has characters ranging from Smokey the Bear to Pogo Possum. A comic-strip character created by the late Walt Kelly, Pogo was as popular in the 1950s as Dooly is in Korea now. Pogo actually ran for president but lost to Dwight D. Eisenhower. Nonetheless, every four years a "Pogo for President" campaign begins again.

But my favorite animals are cats - including tigers. And what better place for tiger tales than Korea? Everywhere one looks in Korea is an emblematic tiger. (Among the first things I saw, on arriving in Korea years ago, was a painting of a tiger roaring at the moon.) And bookstores are full of tiger stories. The tiger who was terrified of persimmons ··· the tiger who became an old lady's devoted pet ··· the list seems endless.

Tigers have even left their mark on the Korean language. To indicate that a story happened long ago, Western folk-tales begin, "Once upon a time ···" But Korean folklore says, "When tigers smoked pipes ···"

Hmmm ··· what do you suppose the tigers were smoking in their pipes way back then? Had tobacco somehow found its way from Virginia to Korea?

In that case, there is no mystery why tigers are so rare in Korea today. A three-pipe-a-day habit is enough to send the biggest, strongest cat to the mortuary!

Seoul's Good Guys ⋯ and Gals!

It takes a lot of people to keep a great city running. Let's salute some of the hardy souls who make Seoul a good place to live and visit!

1. **Bus drivers** ： Talk about earning your pay! How would you like to spend your day coping with Seoul's traffic?

2. **Police** ： The Korean cops I'me met have been polite, patient, and professional. It's nice to know they're there!

3. **Taxi drivers** ： They're wonderfully patient with my fumbling attempts to speak Korean.

4. **Ajummas** ： That's the collective word for the middle-aged ladies who preside over shops and restaurants. Three cheers for Ajumma! Long may she reign!

5. **Postal workers** ： How do they deliver all that mail each day, to addresses written in at least two languages? Amazing.

6. **Chefs** ： All that bibimpap doesn't get on the table by

itself, you know.

7. **Waiters and waitresses** ： How many tons of kimchi do you suppose the average waitress carries in a year?

8. **Tourist information specialists** ： Hats off to those knowledgable, articulate folk who tell you how to find what in Seoul. Where would we be without them? (Lost, That's where!)

9. **Tour guides** ： This job takes a rare kind of good humor and patience, and a rare kind of person to do it.

And finally …

10. **The staff** ： These hard-working, all but invisible people empty the wastebaskets, change the sheets, clean the bath-rooms and brew the coffee. They make your vacation or business visit possible.

Applause, please!

The Sticker Society!

About every other morning, something slips out and falls when I open my apartment door.

It's a sticker. It usually advertises a restaurant: chicken, Galbi, or whatever. A cartoon face, such as a grinning pig, accompanies a vivid photo of meat on a plate.

I toss the sticker in the wastecan and wonder how many forests went into making these things. Then another thought occurs to me: is the advertising sticker the REAL emblem of Korea?

Consider other nations' emblems. Canada has the maple leaf. Japan has the cherry blossom. America has a smoking gun. Why shouldn't Korea adopt the advertising sticker?

It has the qualifications for a national emblem. It's everywhere. It's recognizable on sight. And the things it advertises are distinctively Korean – Galbi palaces, bibimbap outlets, and so on.

Also, in its own way, It's a cheerful work of art. A

dancing cartoon cow on an advertising sticker makes you smile. Can one say the same for the humdrum plants, snakes, and carrion birds that represent other lands?

So, how about a national advertising sticker for Korea? A jolly tiger would work fine. At least, I'm put one on MY car!

Podori Patrols!

All over Seoul, you see cartoon characters in police uniforms. One is male, the other female. The cartoon policeman is 'Podori'. The lady's name, I'me never heard. Together, they represent the Seoul Metropolitan Police, whose jurisdiction is the wild, weird wonderland-on-the-Han.

I'me had a few encounters with Korea police, all pleasant. The Korean cops I'me met have been patient, polite and professional. Some seemed downright jolly. When an Incheon policeman stopped me to check my alien identification card, he made a good-humored jest of the proceeding. "Oh!" he said. "Handsome picture!"

The Seoul police are also used to dealing with foreigners. They have shown special patience with this gray-bearded Westerner whose taxi driver once had to stop at a police station for an explanation of my directions. (My spoken Korean is on about the same level as a parrot?)

I wanted to go to Seollung. The driver thought I meant Seoul Station(pronounced 'Seoul-yeok'). The policeman on duty straightened it all out in a jiffy.

I'll admit that cops here are not the cute, big-eyed cartoon waifs depicted by the public relations department. Far from it. These guys mean business. That, I imagine, is one reason the streets are safe at night - at least, vastly safer than in my old neighborhoods in DC and Baltimore.

The Seoul police have also had the wisdom to retain that grand old institution, the cop on the beat. You don't find these fellows in coffee shops munching doughnuts. they're out there patrolling the streets. Watching them, I can't help thinking that a uniformed embodiment of law and order is a nice thing to have marching around the neighborhood.

So, be glad Podori is on patrol! Those brawny boys in blue make the difference between life and death daily, for a lot of people. What's more, Korea's cops are one reason Korea is a civilized nation ··· unlike another part of the globe that I could name!

Adrift in Seoul (and Loving It!)

One night recently, I got lost in Seoul ⋯ and didn't mind a bit.

This happens every few days. My sense of direction is awful. I can lose my way in a phone booth. Moreover, Seoul is easy to get lost in. If you expect a nice neat grid of numbered streets and avenues, as in New York or DC – forget it! Except for a few thoroughfares, Seoul just grew, like ivy. The result is a maze of countless little streets and alleys, some of them barely wide enough to admit a bicycle. So if you make a wrong turn, and you can't see any big landmarks like Seoul Tower, you may find yourself lost.

But don't fret. Just walk. Before long, you'll come to a subway stop, or a park, or a palace. Then you'll know where you are. When I got lost the other evening near Anguk Station, I just strolled along, confident that a subway sign would show up soon. And it did.

Along the way, it was fun to look at the shops. One was

full of lovely Hanbok, Korean traditional clothing. At little restaurants, foods like Mandu and Gimbap were arranged in pretty still-life patterns. (Why does Korean food look so much better than American fare?)

But the most wonderful thing was this: I was walking through one of the world's biggest cities at night, alone, with a fairly large sum of cash in my pocket - and unafraid of assault or robbery!

So if you lose your way, relax! Enjoy it! Getting lost in Seoul is actually a nice way to spend your time!

Superlative Seoul!

Seoul is, without question, the best big city I'me ever lived in. You may disagree. That's your privilege. And other cities do have their charms. San Francisco has beautiful scenery. Rome has the beauty of antiquity. Tokyo has the gorgeous symmetry of Mt. Fuji right next door. And so on.

But for safety, beauty and a special touch of whimsy, Seoul is in a class by itself. Walking down a tree-lined street, you are in minimal danger of assault and robbery. And peering into shops, you get a glimpse of another world.

Pharmacies do business with old-fashioned wooden cabinets. From one store window, a benign portrait of King Sejong looks back at you. And if you turn a particular corner at random, you find yourself on the grounds of a palace that was already generations old when Shakespeare was born.

Granted, there are other nice places in Korea. My students used to rave about 'beautiful Jeju Island' as if it were a terrestrial paradise. So, when business took me there a couple of years ago, I looked forward to seeing this lush piece of real estate.

It was pretty ⋯ at first. The bus ride to the hotel took us through verdant countryside where I recall seeing the last thing I would have expected to see in Korea: a huge St. Bernard dog. But unless you are an avid bicyclist or horseback rider, there really is not much to do at Jeju Island except look at extinct volcanoes and shiver in that cold sea wind. (People in Jeju are kind and hospitable, but the island itself is like the Outer Banks of North Carolina: once you're seen the sea and the sand, There's not much left to see.)

If you love country living, fine. But give me Gangnam any day!

You Never Know Whom you'll Meet in Seoul!

Quick! What's the most important thing to bring on a visit to Seoul?

Traveler's checks? A guidebook? A good pair of walking shoes? Those are important, sure.

But the most important thing is a supply of business cards, because you never know whom you're going to meet!

Chance encounters here are like nowhere else. A foreigner visiting Seoul may meet a Korean CEO when he offers to help you interpret the menu at a restaurant. Then, you'll want to have that business card handy!

Something like that happened to me. A vegetarian friend from Canada took me to dinner at a restaurant near the Sejong Cultural Center. She wished to avoid meat but could not identify meatless dishes on the menu.

A well-dressed man at the next table came to the rescue. He kindly pointed out suitable items on the list. He turned out to be an executive at one of Korea's most important companies!

We exchanged cards, and have remained in touch. An unplanned meeting at a restaurant thus provided a friend high in Korea's corporate world.

Korea is like that. The guy in the blue business suit beside you could be an extremely good person to know!

Not everyone you meet will be a mover and shaker ··· but you will come away with good new friends nonetheless.

That's why you should keep your cards handy. And keep all the cards you receive. They might be the most valuable things you bring home from Korea!

3

THE SURPRISING
UNDERGROUND CITY IN SEOUL

Go Underground

When you visit Seoul, you get two cities in one!

There is the elegant, high-tech city aboveground ⋯ and the bustling, bargain-filled city belowground!

Just walk downstairs into one of the city's countless underground shopping malls, and suddenly - like Alice - you enter a wonderland of shops big and small, packed with anything you might need or desire.

One of my favorite underground shops in Seoul is a used-book store near City Hall. The stock includes everything from classic mysteries to back issues of Mad magazine. Amazing! Another great shop is a record store near my office. A rack near the entrance has a marvelous selection of classical CDs. If you need a dose of Mozart, you can get it, for a modest price.

Hungry? You have your choice of eateries both humble and elegant, Western and Korean, eat in or take out. Fond of Japanese food? It's there. So is an English pub, if I recall correctly. don't forget the bakeries, either! Underground Seoul is full of them, and they are great. I frequent one bakery near Gyeongbokgung that sells an exquisite oatmeal‒raisin bread.

Under the streets of Seoul, you can walk for miles through a vast emporium of wares from East and West. It's all here ⋯ from Aspirin to Zippers, Suits to Sodas, and Hairpins to Hanbok(traditional Korean clothing). Underground Seoul has another fine feature, too: art galleries! They offer traditional Korean paintings at very reasonable prices. Since Koreans are the greatest artists in the world with watercolor, brush and ink, underground shoppers in Seoul have an opportunity to invest in some fine original Korean art ⋯ without breaking one's budget!

So while in Seoul, remember to visit the supercity beneath the streets. Underground Seoul could be the best part of your trip!

Seoul's Subway Symphony!

Visiting Seoul for the first time? Make sure you ride the subway.

That's right. The subway! Seoul's subway is one of the city's great attractions.

It's clean. It's safe. The trains run on time. You do not see scribbled graffiti on every surface.

You can cross the whole city for the price of a canned soda. And the subway spares you from Seoul's notorious rush-hour traffic tieups!

Shopping is another attraction of the Seoul subway. Seoul has combined its subway system with a huge network of underground shopping centers. So if you find yourself absolutely dying for coffee and chocolate croissants while riding the No. 2 line downtown, you probably can find a nice coffee shop only a few steps from a subway exit, in the underground galleries.

Or if you just enjoy window-shopping, there is plenty

of opportunity for that in those long corridors too. One underground shopping center downtown runs parallel to the subway for some two kilometers!

But for me, the most pleasant thing about Seoul's subway is the music. You never know what you may hear next: anyting from Bing Crosby to the Bach - Gounod "Ave Maria" to surfing songs from the 60s.

As you travel by subway, the music may carry you on a nice little nostalgia trip at the same time. That happened to me recently.

As I waited for the Suso train, the station's sound system played 'Fascination'. For a moment, I was back in childhood, in a simpler America, before the upheavals of the 1960s.

So ride the subway. And keep your ears open.

Seoul's subway symphony may reawaken happy memories you thought you had forgotten!

On the Merry Orange Line!

Beneath the city center, in a region subterrine,

Runs the subway train belonging to the merry Orange Line!

Rolling through the heart of Seoul from dawn till after dark,

It skirts the eastern edges of the cheery Jangchung Park.

Past Dongguk U. and Shindang-dong, and pausing at Yaksu,

It rumbles under Donghoro and under Anguk too.

Then a visit at Uljiro, and at Chungmuro as well,

And It's off to Jongno 3-ga, next to Jonggak and its bell.

Now you're in a regal district, as evinced by Jongmyo

And Changdeokgung and Gyeongbokgung and other-gungs you know.

And Gwanghwamun, where haitai on their pedestals recline,

Is another striking sight upon the lengthy Orange Line!

The train progresses northward, on the way to Gupabal,

Past the stately culture center with its mighty concert hall,

And the famous Folk Museum, and the street at Hyojaro,

Not to mention Naejadonggil and its neighbor Sajingno.

There's much that one could to this, like little Sajik-dong,

But I can't continue further, for the page is none too long.

A busy, buried railway, where massive mirrors shine!

Tell me, what's your destination on the merry Orange Line?

Ogden Nash on the Blue Line!

As far as I know, the late American poet Ogden Nash – author of the famous verses for "Carnival of the Animals" and known for his inventive rhymes – never visited Seoul. But if he rode the Seoul subway today, I imagine he might produce a work like this:

Through Seoul the Blue Line
winds its way long and sinuous,
Past many stops between one
and the other terminuous,
Through stations adorned with
well–tended, sparkling aquaria
And escalators and elevators
and other assorted perpendicularia,
Pausing at Myeong–dong
with its countless boutiques,
And Sadang and Sookmyong

and Sungshin Women's U-tiques,
And the bustling student district
at Daehangno,
Site of many a coffee shop
and PC-bang,
All of which should remind us,
as we get off the subway at Hyehwa,
That Seoul was not built
in a dyehwa.

4

THE SONG OF A TIGER

Sejongno Song!

Greatest of boulevards, grandest of streets,
Heart of the city, where everyone meets,
Hub of a vibrant and vast metropole –
you're in Sejongno, the center of Seoul!
City Hall plaza to Gwanghwamun gate,
Coffee shops humble and monuments great,
These are all parts of a colorful whole –
They're in Sejongno, the center of Seoul!
Stop at the palace, its buildings to see,
Walk by the statue of Admiral Yi,
Pause at a bakery, munch on a roll –
All in Sejongno, the center of Seoul!
Bookstores and barbers and vendors galore,
The Cultural Center and endlessly more;
Taxicabs hurtle, pedestrians stroll –
You're in Sejongno, the center of Seoul!

Now, a Word from the Haitai

Afoot by Gyeongbok Palace
On an early morning walk,
One has to wonder what we'd hear
If Haitai learned to talk.
The toothy, fire-eating beasts
Atop their blocks of stone
Might give us quite a lecture in
A basso monotone.
'Seoul's by autos overrun!
Bring back the ox and cart!
And punk and hip-hop, oi and such –
You call that garbage "art"?
At least you're kept the palaces
Intact from ancient days.
Yet how can monuments endure
This photochemic haze?'
On and on and on they'd go,

Lamenting modern times.
So Let's be glad they cannot speak
At all, much less in rhymes!

Wordsworth at the PC-bang!

An e-mail waited to be sent
Upon a summer's day,
And yet my office was at least
A quarter-mile away.
So to a PC-bang I went,
The Internet my goal;
And there, I saw what has become
Of adolescent Seoul.
In games, the children slaughter beasts
Of every shape and size,
The violence reflected in
Their wide, unblinking eyes.
Yet none among them moves an inch,
Or leaps, or jumps, or fidgets;
They sit completely rigid, save
For swiftly clicking digits.
No motion make they now except

To move a mouse along:
Roll'd round in Earth's diurnal course
At someone's PC-bang.

Ten Arms, and What Good Do They Do?

D is for Dried squid, the national snack.

It's never been known to bite anyone back.

It's sold in packets, dessicated,

Munched by the inebriated,

Dried on racks along the shores,

Bought at corner grocery stores,

Obdurate as roofing nails,

Portable in luncheon pails,

Free of any muss or fuss,

And thoroughly ubiquitous.

Squids cavort with schools of whiting,

But when a boat festooned with lighting

Sets upon them with a fury,

Squids recite their morituri,

Kick the bucket, buy the farm,

Lay down every tenfold arm,

And soon are hung, one after one,

To toughen in the noonday sun.
A squid, when dried, is like a kite,
Broad and thin and stiff and light,
But, far from soaring to the skies,
Winds up among the merchandise,
And there, though unspectacular,
Becomes a treat tentacular.

A-Bridged

Seoul's river is the Hangang, and on its banks you'll see
The National Assembly hall and lofty 63,
And close at hand, the noble spans of bridges seventeen:
Cheonho and Gimpo at the ends, and others inbetween.
These arteries across the waves are sturdy, straight, and
true:
Haengju, Songsan, and Yanghwa to Jamshil and Songsu.
How close they're tied the Gangnam side to busy Itaewon,
And everyone to everything that Seoul depends upon!
The water streams past Dongho Bridge, past Hannam
and Oksu,
And when it comes to Wonhyo Bridge, the river splits
in two.
Past Yoido's two banks it flows, majestic and carefree,
Then reunites at Seogang for its journey to the sea!
Just like the ancient capital with which it shares its fame,
The river is a changeless thing that never stays the same!

This puzzle is a paradox to contemplate as you
Sit back, relax along the shore, and revel in the view!

A Kat IS a Hat in Korea!

Apologies to Dr. Seuss! His famous fantasi-a,
The Cat in the Hat, sounds funny here,
For a kat(Gat)* IS a hat in Korea!

A kat is a hat, a kat is a hat,
A kat is a hat in Korea!

That stubby little horsehair hat, tied tight beneath the chin,
Once perched atop the noggins of Korean gentlemen.
And surely as the rising sun upon the morn will see ya,
A kat can't be inside itself,
For a kat IS a hat in Korea!

A kat is a hat, a kat is a hat,

---

* kat(Gat): Traditional Korean hat

A kat is a hat in Korea!

But Let's not pick on Dr. Seuss, who surely didn't see
A kat inside itself is an impossibility.
The kat that sat so stat-ic on the head in histori-a
Is what they wore in days of yore:
A kat IS a hat in Korea!

A kat is a hat, a kat is a hat,
A kat is a hat in Korea!

Hanbok, Hanbok Everywhere!

Hanbok[*] is Korean dress,
Hanbok is tradition, yes,
Hanbok is historic wear,
Hanbok, Hanbok everywhere!
Hanbok, never out of style,
Hanbok, bold and versatile,
Hanbok, simple, clean and bright,
Hanbok, morning, noon, and night!
Hanbok, made for special days,
Hanbok, made in countless ways,
Hanbok, worn in days of yore,
Hanbok in a modern store!
Hanbok ancient, Hanbok new,
Hanbok green and white and blue,
Hanbok here and Hanbok there −
Hanbok, Hanbok everywhere!

---

[*] Hanbok: Korean traditional costume

Sing Jindo, Jindo, Jindo!

Jejudo has its ocean winds,
Volcanic hills and hogs,
And right next door to Jeju is
The island of the dogs!

Sing Jindo, Jindo, Jindo!
Let canines stand agog!
A thundering crescendo
For Korea's famous dog!

His keen and moistened nostrils
The salty air inhale,
While at the other end he wags
A bushy, curling tail!

Jindo, Jindo, Jindo,
A dog to recommend-o!

Sing Jindo, Jindo, Jindo,
Without diminuendo!

Behold the stalwart Jindo,
Whose stamina astounds!
So brave and independ-o,
These furry, sturdy hounds!

Jindo, Jindo, Jindo!
Let every travelogue
Tell all about this endo-
Genous Korean dog!

Halmeoni, Halmeoni!

Halmeoni*, Halmeoni, 80 or more,

Halmeoni, Halmeoni, witness to war,

Diminutive package of wrinkles and bones,

Adrift in an era of cellular phones!

Halmeoni, Halmeoni, silver of hair,

Halmeoni, formerly fairest of fair,

Halmeoni, working the garden alone,

How many grandchildren call you their own?

Halmeoni, Halmeoni, what are their names?

Do they talk about aught but their video games?

And did you imagine, in 1972,

The world that one day would be waiting for you?

Halmeoni, Halmeoni, idle at last,

Halmeoni, Halmeoni, lost in the past,

How does it feel to be bodily hurled

Into a 21st-century world?

---

* Halmeoni: a grandmother

Lost in a Bestiary!

The snakes are in the grasses
And the wolf is at the door,
The bats are in the belfry
And the monster's on the moor,
But where Korean fauna lurk,
I simply cannot say.
Which figures of Korean speech
Involve them every day?
Do 두꺼비-ies (1) flatter bosses?
Is one clever as a 여우 (2) ?
Or as busy as a 비버 (3) ?
And do 생쥐 (4) run up the clocks?
Is one braver than a 사자 (5) ?
Or as slippery as an 뱀장어 (6) ?
Or as noisy as a 까치 (7) ?
Like a 새끼 돼지 (8) does one squeal?
Please, someone lead me out

Of this linguistic hinterland!
I'm as helpless as an 타조 (9)
With its head beneath the sand!

1. toad
2. fox
3. beaver
4. mice
5. lion
6. eel
7. magpie
8. piglet
9. ostrich

The Seoul ABC!

A is for Ajumma, doughty and strong,

B is for Bibimbap, had for a song,

C is for City Hall, solemn and gray,

D is for Daehwa, out Jengbalsan way,

E is for Ehwa, the great Woman's U.,

F is for Fried Fish(or samchi to you),

G is for Gangnam, an affluent space,

H is for Hanbok all over the place,

I is for Icheon, the pottery site,

J is for Jonggak, so busy at night,

K is for Kwanghwamun, gate for the ages,

L is for Learning of SNU sages,

M is for Mok-dong, beside Omokgyo,

N is for Namdaemun Market aglow,

O is for Oksu, the river beside,

P is for Baeksok, a long subway ride,

Q is for Questions("Which way's Dongnimmun"?)

And Quaint sidewalk vendors at work in the sun.

R is for Rice bowls on restaurant tables,

S is for Shoppers perusing the labels,

T is for Dongdaemun, landmark supreme,

U is Uljiro, crowded to an extreme,

V is for Victory by Admiral Yi,

W ⋯ hmm ⋯ that must be Wangshimni,

X means the X-cellent shops in Yongsan,

Y is for Yatap, next door to Moran,

Z is for Zoo, where the animals run,

And That's all there is, for the alphabet's done!

SEOUL, 'THE MIRACLE WONDERFUL'

Delightful Dawns!

Every city has its best time of day ⋯ the hour when everything is most beautiful. Here in Seoul, It's just before dawn, preferably on a chilly autumn day, with a few wispy cirrus clouds high overhead glowing pink in the sun's earliest rays.

Get a cup of coffee from a vending machine on the street. Then just stroll around a neighborhood like Yeoksam-dong, where I live now.

All around are the sounds of a great city coming to life. Something nearby starts playing the 'Minute Waltz.' It may be a delivery truck, warning bystanders that It's backing up. (Sometimes a vehicle in reverse makes a memorable tableau. I recall seeing two hulking ROK soldiers squeezed into a tiny sedan that was nonchalantly playing 'Home Sweet Home.')

Street vendors are out early, selling everything from newspapers to bean-paste cakes shaped like fish. Try those cakes, by the way. They are a tasty and inexpensive way to start the day.

Already, children are on their way to school. Korean schoolkids keep the longest hours of any on earth. And 'Ajumma'(auntie), the collective name for the middle-aged ladies whose labors keep Seoul running, has been up for hours, setting up storefront displays of everything from beef to berries.

Delivery men on motorbikes putter down side streets, tossing newspapers that land with a soft WHAP! on doorsteps. Somewhere, a doorbell plays 'American Patrol.' And as the sky lightens, the tall buildings around you turn from silhouettes of sable into palisades of pink.

Seoul at daybreak is a lovely show – and free of charge. Enjoy it while you're here!

It's Like This, Admiral Yi ...

We all know that statues don't really come to life. But anything can happen in the imagination, so I'm free to tell you about my imaginary encounter with Admiral Yi Sun-shin.

You can't miss the Admiral. His statue looms over the street near the Ministry of Culture and Tourism. And one evening as I walked home from work, a subterranean voice thundered: "YOU THERE!" (Pause) "Yes, YOU! With the long nose and gray beard! Where on earth did YOU come from?" "America", I said, wondering if my 30-year-old US Air Force ROTC salute would mean anything to the Admiral. "Never heard of it", Admiral Yi said. "It's a distant land where large numbers of people get drunk every July 4 and kill one another on the roads", I explained. 'Interesting', the Admiral said, and hopped down from his pedestal, landing with an earth-shaking jolt. "What do you do here?' he inquired. 'I'm in the television business".

"Tele ⋯vision?"

"It sends moving pictures through the air. It also urges people to spend money they don't have on things they don't need."

Admiral Yi shook his head. Then he pointed at a man nearby. 'What's THAT' 'he roared.

"It's ⋯ um ⋯ a young man with long purple hair and earrings", I replied.

The Admiral touched the hilt of his sword, and I wondered if the kid's head was about to roll. But the Admiral sighed instead and said, "Oh, never mind. Where is a good restaurant?"

"Across the street and turn left", I answered. "Watch out for the traffic!"

But my warning was needless. Could any mere automobile stop Yi Sun-shin? Kicking cars out of his way with a crash and screech of metal, his huge figure plowed across the street and disappeared into the night.

Say Hello to Ajumma!

Who keeps Seoul running?

Police, firemen, doctors, garbage men, cooks, electricians, carpenters: they, and many others, do their part to keep the Dynamo-on-the-Han humming.

But ultimately, Seoul depends on one lady ⋯ Ajumma!

Her name is pronounced 'ah-joom-mah'. It means Auntie. you're seen Ajumma. She's the sturdy, compact, middle-aged lady who presides over stores. She also brings those heaping trays of food to your table at restaurants. She sweeps floors and cuts hair. She sells everything from newspapers to toy dinosaurs.

Is there anything Ajumma can't and doesn't do? She was performing 'multi-tasking' long before computer geeks began talking about it!

Ajumma works fantastically long hours. Before dawn, she is setting up her fruit stand in the outdoor market near my home. And far into the night, in snow or steamy weather,

Ajumma is on duty, selling everything from kimchi to chewing gum.

Moreover, Ajumma has the muscular strength of a linebacker, in a body barely five feet tall. She lifts loads that would throw my back out!

Seoul couldn't exist without Ajumma. Other people make headlines, but Ajumma is the quiet caryatid on which the city rests.

Here is my favorite Ajumma story. One day I was walking down the street and heard someone call out. I turned and saw Ajumma running toward me. In her hand were two 1,000won notes. I had overpaid on a purchase the previous day, and she wanted to make sure the money was returned. It is hard to imagine that happening in DC or New York.

So, do something nice for Ajumma! Her tireless labors make your cozy visit to Korea possible!

Egg-stensive Eggs!

Sometimes I wonder why every third object I see in Seoul is an egg.

That's scarcely an exaggeration. Everywhere I go, an egg turns up before me.

At the convenience store, a bowlful of eggs sits on the front counter. At the public bath, a small carton of eggs stands on a table next to the TV set. (Why the eggs are at the bath is uncertain. I'me never actually seen anyone there eat one.)

On the streets of Seoul, one encounters eggs en masse. Trucks loaded with eggs roll down the street. Motorcycle delivery men haul teetering towers of packaged eggs to groceries or restaurants or wherever. This is an impressive balancing act. It makes juggling chainsaws look easy by comparison.

At restaurants, my egg allergy forces me to scan the menu carefully for something egg-less. That's not always easy to find. Often, I just give up and go with samchi (grilled mackerel). They haven't found a way to slip egg into THAT yet!

It all makes you wonder. Dinosaurs laid eggs. Once, we are told, dinosaurs ruled the planet. But then they vanished, almost overnight. Do you suppose all their eggs were stolen for …?

Naw. Korean history couldn't go back THAT far!

Surreal Signs!

One of the most delightful things about Korea is Konglish, that hybrid of English and Korean that almost everyone speaks. Koreans apologize for it. But I think It's great! Who wants to use boring Britglish or antiseptic Ameringlish when colorful Konglish is around?

Something curious happens to the English language as soon as it enters Korean airspace. Adjectives acquire new meanings. Direct objects drop off and disappear (possibly to the same place odd socks go). Verbs ⋯ well, diversify.

And so, you get signs like:

- **Beettle Beer** : After seeing that one, I imagined seeing a bug stagger across my desktop, squealing 'HAPPY NEW YEAR!' 'Flash Baekery?' Is there magnesium powder in the cookies?

- **Alram Beel** : No, That's not an Arabian oasis. It's Konglish for 'Alarm Bell'. Then there are the T-shirts. Sometimes their mottoes look as if stirred with a spoon.

One reads, 'UFO. Meeting Next Particular Any Style or Color'. That makes about as much sense as anything about UFOs!

Another T-shirt says simply, 'Fiend', Le's hope That's just a misspelling of 'Friend' And the back of someone's jacket urges, 'Just Take Care Of'. That's all. No object. Open-ended advice! What a concept!

Looking at Konglish signs, you feel freed from all those stodgy rules of grammar and spelling that bored you so in school. It's the linguistic equivalent of bungee jumping.

Away with rules, says Konglish! Play volleyball with verbs, and polo with pronouns! And let the participles fall where they may!

Is That a Giant Bowling Pin?

Koreans call their country 'the Land of Morning Calm?'. I tend to think of it as 'the Land of Inverse Proportions'. What is big in the West becomes small here, and vice versa.

Consider automobiles, for instance. The Korean 'limousine' is a sedan by American standards. The Korean 'mansion' would be a typical suburban home in the United States or Canada.

At the other extreme, tiny things in the West become colossal in Korea. Not far from my office, for example, is a gigantic golden sculpture of a toad. If the thing were alive, it could swallow a helicopter with one gulp.

And then there is the giant bowling pin. Up to five meters tall, it looms by the dozens above the skylines of Korea. It advertises indoor bowling lanes, and brings to mind a moonship ready for launch.

In many ways, Koreans think small. Diminutive engravings, tiny shops, near-microscopic cars … all these

things are distinctively Korean.

But when Koreans think big, they think REALLY big. No middling measures for these people. When they build a ship, It's a supertanker. And when they make a bowling pin, it looks like a payload for the space shuttle.

So if you happen to see a bowling pin big enough for Paul Bunyan outside your hotel window, don't worry. you're not hallucinating. You just happen to be in the only land I know where one can give directions by saying, "Turn right at the giant bowling pin …"

Stop and Watch the Fish!

Every big city, it seems, has characteristic animals. Rome has cats. Moscow has ravens. New York has rats and poodles.

And Seoul has fish. Lots of fish, in ponds and aquaria all over the city.

Sometimes It's hard to turn around without finding yourself looking straight at a beautiful fish. One bank near my office has an outdoor pond. During the warm months, the pond is full of huge ornamental carp.

They have a fantastic range of hues, from an unearthly silver-gold to a deep rich blue-gray. People pause and watch them. They throw coins into the pond. I wonder what the fish think about this rain of metal.

On the way home at night, I pass seafood restaurants with aquaria in their windows. The fish here are for food, not aesthetics, but they're nice to watch anyway.

One restaurant near my home used to have a handsome shark, about a meter long. How did they keep the shark from eating other fish in the tank? I never figured that out.

Then, one day, the shark was gone. It must have become someone's dinner. I felt sad. It was as if an acquaintance had moved away without saying goodbye.

Seoul is the only city I know where you will even find fish in the subway. That's right. In the subway.

At the Gwanghwamun and Uljiro 1-ga stations, there are big aquaria full of ornamental fish. Amid the bustle of the subway, It's calming to stop and watch the fish for a moment.

The fish don't push and shove. They don't sprint down the platform. They are tranquil and unhurried.

Do you suppose they are trying to tell us something?

Colorful Characters!

Think of Seoulites, and you probably imagine a whole city full of blue-suited salarymen and neatly dressed office ladies, marching off to work in the morning and home again at night. Well, There's some truth in that image. But Seoul has its colorful characters too. Here are a few of them:

- **The Sign Man** : This elderly gentleman roams the subway with hand-lettered signs pinned all over his clothing. He delivers an energetic speech to the passengers, who go right on reading their newspapers as if he doesn't exist. Does he ever get discouraged? Apparently not.

- **Linus** : If you recall the old TV cartoon character 'Linus the Lionhearted', you have some idea how this fellow looks. He sports a huge mane of black hair and wanders through Jonggak and Insa-dong. His clothing looks used, to put it politely. I'me never heard him speak a word. Sometimes I wonder if he actually has 20 billion won stashed in a mattress at home.

- **Mr. Oh** : Short for 'Oh-blivious.' He used to spend the day sprawled on a bench near the office where I worked. Beside him stood his trusty soju bottle. He looked as if he hadn't felt any pain since the 1988 Olympics.

- **The Sock Girl** : She sneaked into our office building one day and tried to sell (I think) cheap socks which I really didn't need. When I said no, her lower lip protruded, and she looked as if about to dissolve in tears. Then she vanished, hosiery in hand. I hope she isn't telling all of Seoul that Americans have hearts of carborundum.

That's all for now. Maybe someday I'll tell you about the Dinosaur Lady, the Motorcycle Man, and the Spontaneous Hugger!

Kimchi Cornucopia!

My late mother, a North Carolinian devoted to Southern cooking, would have been fascinated to visit her son in Seoul. But I can imagine her reaction on encountering kimchi, Korea's spicy dish of pickled vegetables.

"You eat THAT?!" Mom would say.

Well, yes. It's tasty and nutritious. Besides, you can't avoid kimchi in Korea. Visiting Seoul without eating kimchi is like skin diving without getting wet. It's unthinkable.

Kimchi is a cuisine, an art, and an institution, all in one dish. And Korea is a cornucopia of kimchi. There must be thousands of varieties, based on cabbage, pickles, and anything else you can imagine.

Or almost anything. I'me never seen cactus kimchi. But conceivably, someone in Seoul is working on it!

Mom probably would have gotten used to kimchi. After all, this is South Korea ⋯ so kimchi is Southern cooking too!

Notes on a Dinner Menu

Take a stroll in downtown Seoul,
And most assuredly
You'll find your fill of shops that grill
The creatures of the sea.
And as you pass, through dewy glass
Within a tank you'll spy
The calm and benevolent,
Gray-as-an-elephant,
Elegant octopi!

They sport with special vigor as
They splash and swirl and swoop,
Without a care that dinner fare
They'll be, with rice and soup.
Absent that news, they swim and snooze
In view of passersby:
The highly methodical,

Cephalopodical,
Edible octopi!

These timid beasts possess the least
Defenses one could name;
And whether munched by fish for lunch
Or humans, end the same.
That's what they get, reclusive set,
For always being shy:
The ever-so-succulent,
Never-be-truculent,
Esculent octopi!

The Solid Gold Shark!

Look in the tank at a seafood restaurant, and you may see a shark. Not a fearsome beast like the one in Jaws, but instead a modest little fellow about a foot long, with brown skin mottled like camouflage paint.

He rests glumly on the bottom. His snout moves slowly up and down, as if sniffling from a cold. He looks like the Willy Loman of the sea. But don't underestimate him! you're looking at the Solid Gold Shark!

When I first saw this fish, I thought a one-shark dinner might cost about US $10. After all, there couldn't be more than a few bites of meat on that lean little body. But a Korean friend corrected me. "That shark'll set you back about 100,000 won", he said.

Nearly US $80 for one fish?! I must have looked astonished, because he explained this nondescript little shark is a delicacy. "It's sliced and served raw, sushi style", he said. And each slice, I imagine, represents a 1,000won bill!

Big value comes in small, drab packages, I reflected later. So what'll happen to that forlorn little fish with the big price tag on its tail? Probably it'll become someone's expense-account dinner.

What you'll find on my plate instead is samchi – something like grilled mackerel. It's tasty, and a bargain at about US $5. So you may want to go for the grilled fish, and leave the Solid Gold Shark to those who can afford it!

Eight-armed Entertainment!

Seoul's seafood is great. No doubt about that. But it can also be entertaining. And nothing in the tanks at seafood restaurants is more fascinating to watch than the octopi.

Westerners in general do not have a high opinion of octopi. The octopus is seen as a sinister, ravenous beast waiting to devour swimmers, ships, and even whole cities. (Remember the animated octopus demolishing San Francisco in that classic horror movie It Came from Beneath the Sea?)

Well, That's not how things work in Seoul. Here, people devour octopi, not the other way around. But eating octopus is like chewing on a garden hose. Octopi are more interesting to watch than to eat.

There is plenty of opportunity to watch octopi in Seoul. Tanks in front of seafood restaurants are full of them. And the octopi are more entertaining than anything else in view.

Fish just swim around. Squids are barely more than seagoing fountain pens. But octopi swoop, splash, dive, entwine, and even fight, rearing up and confronting each other like two circus tents having a wrestling match.

Something about octopi reminds me of cats. Their long, slender arms are almost as expressive as a cat's tail. And like a cat, an octopus will curl up in a tight little ball as it sleeps. On awakening, an octopus may even stretch in an almost feline fashion.

Once I saw an octopus curled up on an aquarium floor, apparently agitated. Its arms whirled in tight coils like the gears of a machine. Then it hauled itself up on its legs and stretched. Did it have a bad dream? I wouldn't be surprised.

So stop and peer into a restaurant aquarium during your stay in Seoul. You may become pre-octopi'd! (This is the worst pun I have ever written.)

Green Thumb City!

One reason I like Seoul is that it has lots of parks. For a metropolis, Seoul has green space galore. you're never far from a park, or at least a shaded boulevard.

But There's another reason too. I just don't have a green thumb. On the contrary, I have the negative equivalent of a green thumb. With animals – cats, dogs, birds, fish, chameleons – I'm great. But the plants I buy are doomed.

I remember especially a handsome broadleaf plant that I bought for my office in the US years ago. Watered regularly, bathed in sunlight, it still expired. I sat there sadly watching it depart this world, one leaf at a time. At last, I tossed the bare stalk into the trash bin. Even now, a barren little flower pot stands on my desk where a spring of something fought the odds and failed.

So It's nice to be surrounded here by people who can make things grow. What is more, Seoulites can make plants grow in the most unlikely places. In the middle of Jonggak

one day, I looked up and saw a tiny garden – about two square meters – that someone had fenced in and made to thrive. If you can do that in Jonggak, you can do it anywhere.

So get out and enjoy the gardens, parks, and all the other greenery of Seoul, while warm weather beckons. Seoul is one of the few big cities where a short subway ride will take you from the workplace to the woods!

Cactus Country!

Wild West enthusiasts won't find tumbleweeds in Seoul ⋯ but will find lots of cacti!

In flower shops and convenience stores, you find cacti sitting in tiny terra-cotta pots. Cacti seem to like it here. Maybe Korea's spicy cooking reminds them of Mexico!

Some places have cactus gardens to delight the eye. In a container about the size of a tea tray, you may see a whole community of cacti, sporting red and yellow flowers and an intimidating array of spines.

There used to be an impressive cactus garden on the counter at a post office downtown. All it needed was a horned toad or two.

Of course, only the tiniest horned toad could live in a Korean cactus garden. But maybe Koreans have that problem solved. they're managed to reduce cars almost to microscopic size. Why not wildlife as well?

There is one place where I don't recall ever seeing cacti:

in a restaurant. Perhaps There's a reason for that. After diners have one round of soju too many, you shouldn't let them near anything sharp!

Cell Phone City! (I)

Apart from the long nose, green eyes, and pale skin, I look like any other blue-suited salaryman in Seoul ⋯ with one exception. I don't carry a cell phone.

"Gasp!" (I hear you cry.) "A Seoulite without a cell phone? How do you communicate? What if someone needs to call you? You might be out of touch with the rest of the world!"

Well, that suits me fine. Anyone who really needs to reach me can call me at the office, or knock on my front door. If you can't reach me that way, then the business can probably wait.

You see, Seoul's emblem - the tiger - is a big cat. And living here, I'me become something like a big cat myself. There are times when I don't care to be bothered. Just let me climb up a nice tall tree in the forest, stretch out on a limb, and purr in relief at escaping the rest of the world for a while. That's why tigers and I don't carry cell phones.

Granted, at times I do feel a bit out of touch with the times. When everyone around me is jabbering into those little plastic boxes, I feel like a relic from the days of King Sejong. But I also feel less harried, and spare myself some peculiar situations.

Once, for example, I saw a man in Sajik-dong squatting on the pavement, apparently shouting at an innocuous spot on the asphalt. I wondered if he was deranged. Then I saw he was having an intense exchange over a cell phone.

Besides, do cell-phone users have any idea how they sound? I don't mean the shouted conversations. I mean the tunes those gadgets play. Is ANY conversation so important that it must be heralded by the '1812 Overture?' I know of one man in the US who was actually shot for a lesser disturbance of the peace.

So I'm temporarily out of contact. So what? The world can do without me after office hours. Now, if you'll excuse me, There's a cozy tree limb waiting.

Purrrrr ⋯

Cell Phone City! (II)

During the recent strike by doctors, I wondered: what happens if someone in Seoul needs surgery to have a cell phone removed from his or her ear?

The cell phone has become part of Seoulites' anatomy. If I saw a young person without a cell phone, I would wonder if I had strayed into the wrong country.

Moreover, the cell phone has extended the Korean office everywhere. My employer gave me a cell phone so that I would never be out of touch with my boss. can't predict when a document may need revisions on Saturday!

Practically all of Korea is wired in similar fashion. Once I saw a man apparently shouting at a spot on the pavement. I wondered if he were mentally ill. Then I saw his cell phone.

Sometimes the cell phone indicates social status more reliably than anything else. I seem to recall seeing a forlorn woman seated in a doorway. She looked impoverished and in the direst straits. Had her family abandoned her?

Evidently not. She took out her cell phone and started a conversation. It was like seeing Oliver Twist go online.

The only time Seoul's cell phones trouble me is when the caller is driving.

Possibly, my last sight on earth will be a Seoul motorist roaring toward me ··· cell phone in one hand, cigarette in the other, and the steering wheel unattended!

You Know you're In Seoul When …

What makes Seoul different from other big cities around the world?

You know you're in Seoul when …

You find yourself in a spotless taxi on a clean street.

The subway is unvandalized.

You look up and see a giant bowling pin.

A fire-eating monster with a big toothy grin is an everyday sight.

Half the food on the table is bright red.

You stop to watch a shark in the tank at a seafood restaurant.

A cartoon turtle smiles at you from a construction site.

Pears are almost as big as bowling balls.

Ginseng is everywhere.

Someone giving directions tells you, "Turn right at Admiral Yi."

A coffee shop looks like the lobby of a luxury hotel. People ask you where you teach.

Seoul is clean and colorful, fast and friendly, 21st-century and traditional. Is this a great city, or what?

Seoul Statistics!

Some of the most interesting reading in these parts is 'Facts About Seoul', a publication of the Seoul Metropolitan Government. This little book's figures provide a fascinating portrait of one of the world's greatest cities.

For example, the 2016 edition indicates that every day, in Seoul ⋯

- 206 persons are born, 119 persons die, 157 couples marry, and 49 couples are divorced. (Nothing is constant but change!)
- 7.80 million people ride the subway, 4.28 million ride buses. (At least a million must get stuck in traffic!)
- 76 cars are registered. (Notice how Korean cars are spotless?)
- The average person consumes 303 liters of water. (Much of it goes to wash those spotless cars!)
- The city uses about 127,000 megawatt-hours of electricity and 135,000 barrels of oil. (Petroleum, not

sesame oil!)

- Approximately 11,000 foreign tourists visit the city, and there are 17 fires and 937 incidents of crime. (That's not cause and effect!)

If all this activity tires you, visit a nice quiet coffee shop and relax. Seoul must have at least 100,000 of those!

NONETHELESS, SEOUL & ITS PEOPLE-NOT UNDERSTANDABLE

Enigmatic Encounters!

When East meets West in Korea, many encounters are hard to explain. One gentleman in Incheon, for example, used to hug me whenever he saw me. I don't know why. I never even learned his name.

Then there was the young lady who approached me in a Seoul bookstore and held up a card with the word 'hernia' written on it. I tried to explain the condition. She giggled. I gave up and politely took my leave.

Was she just having fun with a foreigner, or was this some kind of field research in sociology? Maybe my behavior contributed to someone's master's thesis.

One day downtown, a well-dressed young man hailed me by name. Must be a former student, I thought. But why couldn't I recall his name and face?

He asked if I was still teaching at a prominent language school in Seoul. "I didn't teach there", I replied. "I taught in Incheon." He looked puzzled. "Then how do I know

you?" he asked. How indeed?

Finally, there was the tall young Korean man, dressed like a fashion model, at Gyeongbokgung subway station one night. He looked me over for a moment, then gave me a solemn military-style salute and proceeded slowly up the stairs.

My only military experience is one year as an inept Air Force ROTC cadet in college, some 30 years ago. How did I merit a salute? Another mystery of the inscrutable East, I suppose!

Desperately Seeking Shakespeare!

In Seoul, perfect strangers walk up to me and ask advice about things Western. They may want guidance on writing a letter in English, or an explanation of something in Time magazine.

Then there was the man seeking Shakespeare. Not just any Shakespeare, but the complete Shakespeare.

He approached me in a bookstore downtown and said, "You look like a cultured man." I didn't perform my great impression of Curly Howard.

"Can you help me find the complete works of Shakespeare?" he asked.

"I'll try." I replied.

"Is this complete?" he said, holding up an anthology of four plays.

Not quite, I told him.

We checked the store's inventory and found no complete collection of Shakespeare. So I referred him to another bookstore. He thanked me, and we parted company.

If he found the book, then I can only wonder what he made of that stage direction in The Winter's Tale: 'Exit, pursued by a bear.'

Bears won't pursue you here, but you may have encounters like this one. Be patient, and help if you can. It's all in a day's work for a foreigner in Seoul!

Pampered Pups!

If I had to pick the most pampered, cosseted and coddled animal on the planet, it would probably be a pet dog in Seoul.

Among the first sights that greeted me in Korea was a young woman riding the subway, carrying a little white puppy on her lap. Then another lady and dog appeared ⋯ and another ⋯ and another.

I marveled. Cats are my specialty, and taking a cat on an excursion like this would be gory, if not impossible. Sensory overload − noise, light, odors − would freak Kitty so badly that it would take hours to extract her claws from my bleeding arm. The dogs, by contrast, took it all in stride, like rail commuters between Baltimore and DC Soon I found that dogs accompanied their mistresses everywhere − even into restaurants, where once a miniature Schnauzer tried to entice me, with soulful gaze, into giving him a handout. (He failed.) It's not that I dislike dogs they're nice pets. A dog is like a person with a limited education and a peculiar way of leaving his signature. He's pleasant company. Just don't ask him to cosign anything.

Anyway, Seoul is something of a utopia for little domesticated dogs. A few days ago, I saw a middle-aged lady walking down the street near Shinsa-dong, cradling her precious pup in her arms as if it were a favorite child. The scene was touching and slightly unsettling at the same time. I'me known people who lavished attention on pets, and those same people tended to be proportionately short on compassion for other humans.

But in such cases, you can't blame the dogs. And they leave you with unforgettable memories. Outside the corner grocery near my apartment one evening, I found a shaggy little mixed-breed - perhaps the store owner's pet - curled up in a cardboard box.

I paused and peered down at him. Unintimidated, the puppy looked up with big brown eyes as if to say, "Do you have an appointment?"

Forbidden Floors!

In tall office buildings where I've worked in Seoul, two floors have been missing: the fourth and the thirteenth. Thereby hangs a little story of what happens when Eastern meets Western superstition ⋯ and buildings must be adjusted as a result.

It happens that in this part of the world, the word for 'four' sounds like the word for 'Death'. Understandably, no one wants to work on the Death Floor.

So when you get on the elevator in a high-rise building, don't be surprised if the elevator goes straight from the third floor to the fifth. The fourth floor just isn't there.

(The same principle applies, by the way, when you give gifts. DON'T, whatever you do, give someone a four-pack of something. It's roughly like presenting an invitation from the underworld.)

The superstition about 13 being unlucky is purely Western. But Koreans evidently feel they have to accommodate the fears of their overseas guests. So the architects go to work again and eliminate the 13th floor too. And thus the elevator controls get even more complicated.

Meanwhile, two whole floors of numerous buildings in Seoul have been consigned to some eerie netherworld. Who occupies them There's Ghoulies, ghosties, and things that go bump in the night?

Don't ask me. The paranormal isn't my field. I'm just a mild-mannered public relations man!

Oh, Just Eat the Rice!

It takes an iron stomach t' eat a kimchi stew.

It burns away yer gastric wall and duodenum too.

It's hotter 'n the surface of th' solar photosphere,

An' It's said to have a half-life of a hundred thousand year.

How do Koreans live an' thrive on this corrosive brew?

They're a tougher kind o' people than the likes o' me an' you,

Fer at some unknown moment in their hist'ry neonate,

Their entire body cavity gets lined with armor plate.

Of course, you may not heed my words, and take a sip inside.

You'll wish that yer esophagus was made o' telluride.

You'll turn bright red, an' moan a bit, an' curl upon th' floor,

An' when th' paramedics come, they'll haul you out th' door.

Then, as yer lips and nostrils emit a curl o' fume,
And as th' surgeon's waitin' in th' operatin' room,
I trust that you'll remember my politely warnin' you:
It takes an iron stomach t' eat a kimchi stew.

The Charge of the Health Brigade!

Koreans can be stand-offish when you first meet them. But once they decide they like you, their attentions can be almost overwhelming.

They will do all they can to help you adjust to life in Korea ⋯ and one thing they do is shower you with advice.

Especially, advice on health and food. If I had a dollar for every time I'me been urged to eat or drink ginseng, I would have a fortune to rival Bill Gates's.

Particular fruits and vegetables have their partisans, who urge their favorite foods on me. Eat 12 cherry tomatoes a day! Be sure to eat turnips! Apples! Pears! Mugwort! Kimchi is rich in vitamin C! And so on, indefinitely.

Especially heavy advice is aimed at me, because I am diabetic and have to watch blood sugar carefully. And every Korean, it seems, has special advice for handling diabetes.

"Eat this particular kind of rice!" (My blood sugar soared anyway.) "Avoid canned such-and-such!" (My blood

sugar stayed down, like a sleeping dog.)

Meanwhile, the greasy, artery-clogging food of the West is flooding Korea, turning a generation of lithe young Koreans into walking butterballs. Does anyone besides me see an irony here?

Can't You Kids Slow Down?

Here in my dotage – 48 in Korean years – I move more slowly than a few years before. And often I find Korean youngsters surging by me on the sidewalk, like rapids past a rock in the mountains.

This, I'm told, is the 'bbali-bbali' syndrome. It means 'hurry-hurry' Korean youngsters are so hard-pressed to achieve that they feel the need to use every last second productively.

So they must figure: don't walk – RUN! Preferably, run with a cell phone to one's ear. Let no second go unused! Go for it! NOW!

Watching these kids, I feel a peculiar personal pain. Growing up, I was like them. My childhood and adolescence were bbali-bbali, several times over. Under intense family pressure to reach the top, I did well ⋯ for a while. My honors and awards sparkled on graduation from high school. I took an undergraduate degree with distinction from one of

America's top universities.

And then, midway through a graduate program, I cracked. It took years to put myself back together. A stronger, wiser person could have finished the program with that precious M.A. But I was not that person. Nor, I suspect, are many young Koreans jostling me on the sidewalks and in the subway.

Yes, I know. Korea is Korea, and America is America. But there is a limit to the stress anyone, however strongly motivated, can endure.

So won't Korean kids slow down? If the bbali-bbali culture goes unchecked, I wonder how many of them will wind up dropping from heart attacks before age 30 ··· or from high-rise office windows when they find that success is more elusive and disappointing than they ever imagined.

Creative Korea!

One puzzling thing about Koreans is their frequent moan: 'We're not creative!' I don't like to contradict my gracious hosts, but in this case I have to say: 'You're dead wrong.'

In everything from astronomy to warfare, Koreans have a legacy of creativity to match any other people on earth. To take the most famous example: Admiral Yi Sun-shin invented the ironclad warship centuries before the Monitor and Virginia had their shootout at Hampton Roads. (As a born-and-bred Virginian, I was astonished to find that Admiral Yi had beaten my forbears to that invention by so long!)

In our own time, Koreans have revolutionized everything from the toy industry to software. My computer relies on an antiviral program devised by a Korean. Korean traders have swept the seas.

Meanwhile, Korean artists are light-years ahead of the Westerners who nail scrap lumber together and call it 'sculpture'. By contrast, what I'me seen of American art lately has degenerated until it looks as if someone has been throwing mudballs at a wall.

Here I can't help recalling a particular Western artist who rose to fame by drawing stick figures illustrating trendy themes. The task of filling in the name, I'll leave to you. Yes, stick figures! A Korean artist would have produced some-thing more original, I'm sure.

Art, music, industrial design … you name it, and Koreans are as creative as they come. If only they would recognize it!

A Cautionary Tale

Miss Kim, a leading U.'s alum,
Had South Korea's greenest thumb.
A rose, a phlox, a cabbage row,
She made it grow and grow and grow.

To hasten growth, the lady chose
To bombard plants with Berlioz.
Speakers round each pot would play
A roar of brasses night and day.

The price of ginseng caught her eye,
And bold ambition made her cry:
"Great wealth awaits, if I produce
A ginseng big as Betelgeuse!"

But soon the ginseng plant rebelled.
"No more trombones!" the ginseng yelled.

And from its pot, the massive root
A flying leap did execute.

Miss Kim gave chase, and so, ere long,
The startled folk of Apgujong
Saw her pursue, at lightning speed,
The fleeting and enormous weed.

From block to block they race away
And will, I guess, until the day
They come at last to Yeongdeungpo;
And when they do, I'll let you know.

Meet Miss Lonelyhearts!

One former co-worker of mine in Korea was known as Miss Lonelyhearts. At least, That's what I called her. Miss Lonelyhearts shed a lot of tears in my office while we worked together. She also gave me some idea what goes on among women in a Korean workplace.

A plain young woman, she chose me as her confidant and would drop into my office at times for a weepy recital of woe. Hers was a curious case. She had not been jilted by a fickle boyfriend, not battered by an abusive spouse. Instead, she was low in the pecking order among women at the office. And apparently she got pecked often.

"They tell me I am not beautiful!" she said of her co-workers.

Granted, one was unlikely to see her striding down a catwalk. But she dressed well, did a good job at work, and did not deserve mockery. It cost nothing to listen, so I did. I even kept a box of tissues in the office for her. Otherwise, a river of tears might have flowed down the hall and ruined our mainframe.

Miss Lonelyhearts finally married, or so I understand. Where she is now, I have no idea. Maybe she is living happily with a devoted husband.

Anyway, keep her in mind, because you may encounter your own Miss Lonelyhearts while in Korea. you'll know her when you meet her: a young woman who suffers indignities because she does not match a certain ideal of beauty.

Listen to her. Be sympathetic. Offer encouragement. It's probably something she rarely hears.

And keep a box of tissues handy.

Shamans and Show-offs! (I)

The 'Mudang' or shamaness, is a symbol of Korea. Her colorful clothes and stovepipe hat are as familiar here as the postman's blue uniform in the United States.

Not all mudang are women. Some are men. But the ladies have the business locked down pretty tight. And they have a busy schedule. They may be called on to dedicate buildings, contact spirits, or do all manner of other alleged paranormal business.

Sounds much like America, doesn't it's People all over the US rely on faith healers, amulets, and other such resources to ward off disease, bring good luck, and even (they claim) contact the spirits of the dead.

Actually, the American tradition of shamanism was well established long before the New Age crowd discovered it as a way to wealth. The old familiar 'medicine man' of Native American history was actually a shaman. Part of his job was to haul back souls who supposedly had left the body and gone wandering in the netherworld.

The Koreans probably have been at it a little longer than the American shamans, but their motive is basically the same: to make money as a middleman. Korea's shamans make no secret of being in it for the loot. 'I don't work for cheap', a mudang will tell an assembled crowd. And the spectators dig deep in their pockets for cash.

Well, I suppose It's an easy way to make 100,000 won. But the shaman's tricks are a bit transparent ⋯ and even a casual glance will show there is more superstition than the supernatural about the shamans's performance.

Shamans and Show-offs! (II)

When I taught advanced English conversation at a private school, the talk in class turned one day to the mudang and their work. Students recited the alleged wonders those ladies in the colorful robes perform. They speak with the disembodied voices of the dead. They stand, barefooted and unharmed, on upturned knives. They surrender themselves to possession by spirits. And so on.

Okay, they stand on knives. There would be no great danger if the knives were dull. And even if they are sharp, there are ways to shield the soles of the feet without wearing shoes. Just make sure the sole remains unseen!

"They speak with the voices of the dead!" Oh, come on, people. This particular ruse has been in use since Roman times. The will to be believe is so powerful that almost anyone's voice, sepulchrally distorted, could be passed off as a ghost's. Harry Houdini, the escape artist, specialized in demolishing such frauds.

Possession by spirits? Well, any half-skilled actress can pass herself off as a medium for spirits. Closed eyelids, dramatic gestures of the hands ⋯ It's a simpler recipe than lemonade.

North American shamans have similar tricks. A mere lump of red clay can be used to simulate a 'miracle'. Yet the New Age crowd recoils in shock whenever someone questions the validity of such 'wonders'. Well, I question them. I openly chuckle at them. And I'm do worse than that, if I had a certain noisemaker. (you probably know the one I have in mind)

This is not meant to mock Korea. It's a lovely country, and I'm deeply attached to it. Moreover, America is full of similar mudang-ery. I just don't think There's anything paranormal involved. It's only entertainment. And if you want entertainment, try the Sejong Cultural Center!

7

I DO THIS KIND OF WORK.
ANYWAY SORRY!

The Caption Guy!

Quietly, at a little cubicle in an undistinguished office building in Seoul, a long-nosed, gray-bearded man taps away at a computer, pausing now and then to wonder just what he is supposed to write.

You are familiar with this fellow. Me!

My secret life, if you want to call it that, is to proofread the initial translations of Korean TV-show texts and put them into plain, idiomatic English. In other words, my job is to make sure the captions on Korean shows don't read like those on Hong Kong movies.

You know what I'm talking about. The kind of martial-arts film with dialogue like: "Ho, ho! I will resolutely dissever your head and cast it into rubbish container!"

My co-workers and I try to filter out rhetoric like that before it gets broadcast and generates laughter all over Asia. And every day, we are reminded how ambiguous and difficult the English language can be.

I recall when a minor misspelling turned the name of a fish into an ethnic insult. On another occasion, a misused verb idiom turned a perfectly innocent remark into something unairable. Et cetera, ad nauseam.

This is a recipe for burnout. You always fear missing some super-slip of the English tongue that will send waves of laughter (or worse, rage) rippling around the eastern hemisphere.

So if you find me jumping at unexpected noises these days, or notice my hand trembling as I visit the water cooler ⋯ well, this is how beards get gray!

Dress Up!

Want a surprise? Sit in a coffee shop in Jonggak for an hour or so and watch Western passersby on the street.

What you see, all too often, is a parade of ill-groomed people in cheap, shabby clothing. They dress as if for yard work or a beer party instead of a visit to one of Asia's greatest cities.

Would you tolerate a guest who came to your home wearing rags and generally behaved as a hopeless slob? Of course not!

Yet that is precisely what some visitors from abroad do while in Korea. And while the Koreans' patience is legendary, sometimes I wonder what goes through their minds as they watch grubby foreigners shamble past.

As an American, I shudder to see Americans wandering around Seoul dressed practically in tatters. Some Americans' attire and lack of grooming – disheveled hair, ragged clothes, cheap sandals – make them look almost like cartoon cavemen. One school executive in Seoul recently told me of his disgust with ill-dressed young Western teachers at his institute. "They come in here in tank tops!" he growled.

No one expects you to dress as if for a White House dinner throughout your stay in Korea, but it is still a good idea to dress reasonably well.

It requires no great effort. And it shows respect for your hosts, the Korean people, who take pains with their appearance and will be gratified if you do the same.

Dressing down may be the custom at home, but not here. In other words, if you don't wear a tie, then at least make sure your jeans are clean and intact!

The Inscrutable West!

While growing up in the US, I heard cliches about the 'inscrutable East' and the 'mystic Orient'. Then I got to Seoul and discovered it was about as mystical as a phone book.

Actually, the inscrutability is on the other side. The West is harder to understand than the East!

Want to see something really inscrutable? Look at the English language.

English does not exactly defy logic, but does lead it a merry chase. Consider its spelling, which may have nothing at all to do with pronunciation.

Bernard Shaw had great fun with the vagaries of English spelling. How, for example, would you pronounce the word 'ghoti'? Probably, you would pronounce it like 'goatee'.

Wrong, said Shaw. It's pronounced like 'fish'!

How do you get 'fish' out of 'ghoti'? Easy. There's the 'gh' sound from 'tough'. There's the 'o' sound from 'women'. And There's the 'ti' sound from 'action'. Gh-o-t=f-i-sh!

An absurd example? Perhaps. But English is full of them. And the inconsistency between English spelling and pronunciation is just one of the mysteries of the inscrutable West!

Why More Than One Means Trouble!

My song is not of lovely spring,
Or verdant vistas rural;
Instead, I'll treat that ghastly thing,
The wretched English plural!
It's sometimes not sufficient just
To add an s, you see;
The plural form's a nightmare land
Of inconsistency!
We've trees for tree, and wreaths for wreath,
But multiples of tooth are teeth;
For louse, There's lice, and mouse, There's mice,
But homes are houses, never hice!
The arid West is strewn with cacti,
But knowledge rests on facts, not facti;
It's deer for deer and moose for moose,
But flocks of geese, and not of goose!
So if you ask Korean kids

Who English class have sat in,

The best they'll say for English is,

It's not the frightful Latin!

Oh, for a Prefix!

Tonight my thoughts are focused on
A matter stark and sober.
This pressing question's on my mind:
Are ginkgo leaves bilobar?

Above the streets of downtown Seoul
The ginkgos spread their boughs
As long ago they did above
The farmers and their ploughs.

In autumn, ginkgos change their hue
To yellow as the sun
And drop distinctive two-lobed leaves
Down onto everyone.

Two lobes they have, beyond all doubt.
The prefix is the issue.

Di- or bi-? That question haunts
My tired cerebral tissue.

This point of English usage swirls
Within my weary head
Til a solution comes to mind:
Let's speak Chinese instead.

HO, HO ⋯ NO!

If you listen for a loud "HO, HO, HO!" in Seoul during December, you may be disappointed. This is not exactly Santa's stomping ground ⋯ and, at the risk of sounding like Scrooge, I'm grateful.

One gratifying thing about Seoul is its subdued celebration of Western Christmas. (I say "Western Christmas" because Orthodox Christmas, which I observe, comes about two weeks later and is called Nativity.)

In the US, Christmas merchandise starts going on sale in August. And by October, the crescendo of jingles, carols, and Yuletide racket makes me want to fly to Carlsbad Caverns and hide there. Even bats make better company than chuckling elves and talking reindeer.

Meanwhile, all around are signs of a consumer economy gone wild. One Christmas, a store near my former home in Maryland, known for its tacky window displays, put on sale a toy electric guitar, about as long as one's hand, in a package that showed Santa strumming away.

The toy would occupy a child for perhaps two minutes, then be cast aside. How would you explain a product like this – and the economy that produced it – to someone in, say, Nepal or Uganda?

Christmas excess has swamped America. May it spare Korea!

Here is a proposal. Let Korea, as a nation, hurl Santa's tiny guitar back across the ocean to the consumer-driven country that conceived it.

THEN will be the time to say "Ho, ho, ho!"

이 도서의 국립중앙도서관 출판예정도서목록(CIP)은 서지정보유통지원시스템 홈페이지(http://seoji.nl.go.kr)와 국가자료공동목록시스템(http://www.nl.go.kr/kolisnet)에서 이용하실 수 있습니다. (CIP제어번호: CIP2018002798)

Fun in Every Alley **Seoul Stories**

Written & Illustrated by / David Ritchie

Publisher / Cho Yoo Hyun

Editor / Yi Bu Seob

Designer / Park Min Hee

Published by / Nulbom

Registration Number / Je300-1996-106Ho. 8. 8. 1996

Address / 9, Dongsung 4-gil, Jongno-gu, Seoul, 03084, Korea

Tel / 82-2-743-7784   Fax / 82-2-743-7078

1st edition / 25. 03. 2002

revised edition / 20. 02. 2018

ISBN 978-89-6555-067-9 03840